Bubble Gum, Bubble Gum

by Lisa Wheeler

Illustrated by Laura Huliska-Beith

Megan Tingley Books

LITTLE, BROWN AND COMPANY

New York ❧ Boston

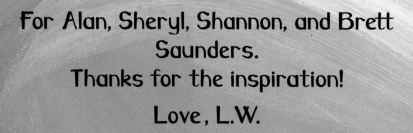

For Alan, Sheryl, Shannon, and Brett
Saunders.
Thanks for the inspiration!
Love, L.W.

For the two newest members of the Huliska
clan: Gabriel and Joseph.
—L.H.B.

Text copyright © 2004 by Lisa Wheeler
Illustrations copyright © 2004 by Laura Huliska-Beith

Little, Brown and Company

Time Warner Book Group
1271 Avenue of the Americas, New York, NY 10020
Visit our Web site at www.lb-kids.com

First Edition

10 9 8 7 6 5 4 3

TWP

The illustrations for this book were done in acrylic
and collaged paper on strathmore paper.
The text was set in Caraway Bold.

Printed in Singapore

Library of Congress Cataloging-in-Publication Data

Wheeler, Lisa.
    Bubble gum, Bubble gum / by Lisa Wheeler ; illustrated by Laura Huliska-Beith.—1sted.
      p. cm.
    Summary: After a variety of animals get stuck one by one in bubble gum melting in the
road, they must survive encounters with a big blue truck and a burly black bear.
    ISBN 0-316-98894-4
    1. Bubble gum—Fiction. 2. Animals—Fiction. 3. Stories in rhyme. I. Huliska-Beith,
Laura, ill. II. Title.
PZ8.3.W5663 Bu 2003
E—dc21
                                     2002016268

Bubble gum,

bubble gum,

Chewy-gooey bubble gum,
Icky-sticky bubble gum
Melting in the road.

Along comes a toad...
A fine, fat toad,
A fine, fat, wild
—SPLAT!—
wart-backed toad.

Ew!
Yuck!

The toad got stuck!

Sticky toad, sticky toad,
Bumpy-icky-sticky toad,
Lumpy, grumpy, sticky toad
Sitting in the goo.

Along comes a shrew...
A bad mood shrew,

A bad mood

—HOW RUDE!—

Tough dude shrew.

Yuck!
Ew!

The shrew's stuck, too!

Gooey shrew, gooey shrew,
Pointy-nose-all-gluey shrew,
Stomping, shouting "**FOOEY!**" shrew

Can't get loose.

Along comes a goose...
A wide, white goose,

A wide, white

—STUCK TIGHT!—

No-flight goose.

Oh!
No!

The goose can't go!

Gummy goose, gummy goose,
Wanted-something-yummy goose,
Sticky, gummy-tummy goose
Can't pull free.

Along comes a bee...
A buzz-buzz bee,
A buzz-buzz
—STUCK FUZZ!—
Bumbled-up bee.

My!
Oh, my!

The bee
can't fly!

Bumble bee, bumble bee,
Roll-around-and-grumble bee,
Pull and kick and stumble bee
Just can't go.

Along comes a crow...
An old, weathered crow,
An old, weathered

—GUM-FEATHERED!—

loudmouthed crow!

Wow!

Oh, wow!
The crow's stuck now!

Talking crow, talking crow,
Loud and loony, squawking crow,
Crying, cawing, shocking crow,
Every feather's stuck!

Along comes a truck...
A big, blue truck,
A big, blue

—COMIN' THROUGH!—

Honk-Honk truck!

Now the crow
And the toad
And the bee
And the goose
And the bad mood shrew
Must chew
And chew

And chew

And chew

And chew

And CHEW!

whew!

Bubble gum, bubble gum,
Light and lifty bubble gum,
Nifty, drifty bubble gum
Floats them toward the sky...

...as the truck zooms by.

One perfect bubble
Bobbles through the air....

Along comes a bear.
A big-bottomed bear,
A big-bottomed

—*SWAT!* GOT 'EM!—

Burly black bear.

POP!
PLOP!

Now the crow
And the bee
And the goose
And the shrew
And the fine, fat toad
Must hide
From the big-bottomed bear
With his nose in the air
And his great, wet mouth
Open wide!

Bubble gum, bubble gum,
Chewy-gooey bubble gum,
Icky-sticky bubble gum,
There's enough to share.

Hey, bear!

Oh, what luck!

The bear got stuck.

Along comes a hen,
A red-ruffled hen ...

Here we go again!